The
Librarian

Steve the Noob

Thank You

Thank you for picking up a copy of my book. I spent many hours putting this book together, so I hope that you will enjoy reading it. As a Minecraft player, it brings me great joy to be able to share my stories with you. The game is fun and entertaining, and surprisingly, writing about it can be almost just as fun. Once you are done reading this book, if you enjoyed it, please take a moment to leave a review. It will help other people discover this book. If after reading it, you realize that you hate it with such passion, please feel free to leave me a review anyway. I enjoy reading what people think about my books and writing style. I hope that many people will like this book and encourage me to keep writing. Thanks in advance.

Special thanks to readers of my previous books. Thank you for taking the time to leave a review. I appreciate it so much; your support means so much to me. I will continue to keep writing and will try to provide the highest quality of unofficial Minecraft books. Thank you for your support.

Check Out My Author Page

Steve the Noob

My Other Books

Diary of Steve the Noob

Diary of Steve the Noob 2

Diary of a Minecraft Centaur

Diary of an Adventurous Steve

Diary of a Not-So-Wicked Witch

Diary of a Cowardly Chicken

Monday 7:00 AM

The sun rose. I just lay underneath the covers embracing the day. Each ray of sun woke me up even more, I didn't need coffee. Who needs coffee? Those who aren't strong enough, that's who. I had tried some of the stuff once and let's just say I'm never supposed to ever have it again.

Not like that has stopped my co-workers from trying to prank me with coffee now and again. Nothing stops the pranksters of Minecraftia.

I got out of my bed and did some simple stretches. I was a librarian, but keeping healthy was still a big part of who I was.

"Orange juice," I muttered under my breath when I went to check the refrigerator.

I had run out and needed to buy some more. Luckily, there was milk to drink this morning. It was decent compared to orange juice, I guess.

Making breakfast was simple and easy. I had all the ingredients for a healthy meal. While eating I looked outside and just took in the view. I was a very simple person with simple tastes. I had no desire to venture outside my village of Craftia and could not understand why others wanted to.

It was silly to dream of adventures in the big world. You'd get uncomfortable really fast and I doubted others really took that into account. Nope, they probably got on a big sugar high and decided to do something stupid. Which probably seemed really smart to them at the time.

I sighed as I cleaned up the kitchen and then got dressed for the day. I had each piece of my clothing laid out and so it was easy to find them and put them on. Looking at myself in the mirror, I held up a fist. Today would be great!

8:00 AM

I stood right outside my house and breathed in the morning air. It was just as sweet as it was every morning. I saw some of my neighbors get out of their own houses, the smell of coffee wafting out. Their eyes were tired and I wondered how everyone wasn't wide awake at the dawn.

The sunrise was beautiful and I would be helping people today. I would be able to help people do research and find books to enjoy on their personal time.

I waved to one of my neighbors and he waved back weakly.

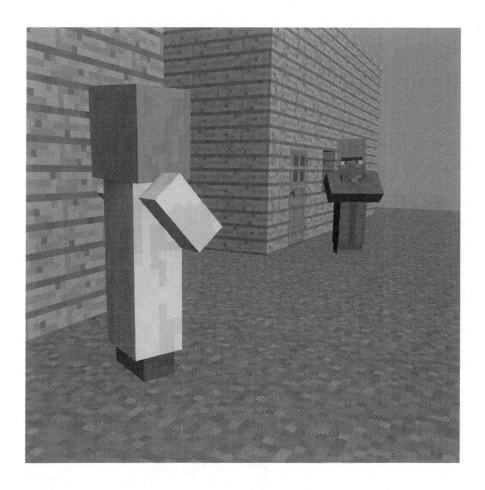

"Good morning," I said as we walked side by side.

"Good," he replied sarcastically. "Morning."

"You're not a morning person?"

"No, I'm not. I'm waking up at the break of dawn to go to a job I don't like."

Looking at his brown robe I saw that he was a farmer. I guess I couldn't really blame him for not liking his job, especially today. The last few days had been extremely hot and he'd be out in the sun. At least I'd be indoors and cool.

"I'm sure you'll be able to manage," I told him, trying to cheer him up.

"Yeah, right," the farmer said, rolling his eyes.

9:30 AM

Walking into the library was a good payoff after the long walk. Okay, I had made it a little longer by taking a long route. In my defense, I had arrived a half hour early so it wasn't like anyone would mind.

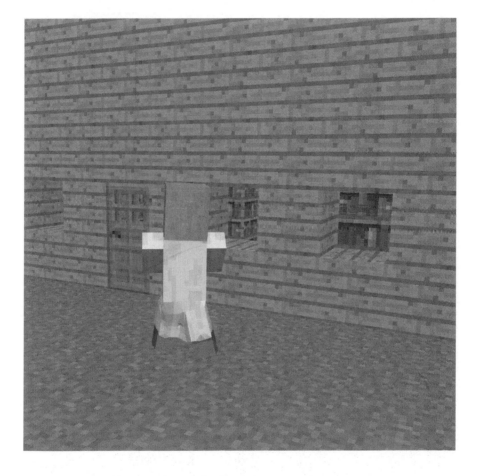

"Jacob, you're here early again."

I turned to see Boss the Head Librarian.

His chest seemed to want to burst out of his white robes and his hand movements were all over the place. This was his usual sign that he was very excited. I smiled, I liked making people happy.

"It's not that hard to do," I told Boss. "I wake up when the sun rises."

"Many people don't," Boss said. "Not without a large cup of coffee and a good paying job. Even then people are still slow to rise."

Yes, people were still slow to rise no matter the benefits. A lot of people turned off the alarm for even five more minutes of sleep. Why waste time in dreams when the world was so wonderful and so vast?

"Glad that I have you on my team," Boss said as he walked towards the fiction section. "Don't know what I'd do without you. Always here early and a clever mind to boot. If only you were more of a people person, you'd be unstoppable."

"I do like people," I told him and looked at the books I was passing.

Books about traveling to far off places on grand adventures. The 'heroes' probably nearly died or were mentally scarred by the end of them. And yet sometimes, these books inspired people to travel from beyond their homes.

It was insane!

"It's just...talking to them is confusing at times," I continued.

"You're just different from most," Boss replied. "Waking up early for one. Not drinking coffee for another."

Now we were passing by the fantasy section. A large, powerful dragon stood on the cover. I shivered and wondered why anyone would want to find a dragon to fight in the first place.

"Doing everything as that is expected of me. Not disappointing the people I work for," I said and Boss nodded, a small smile forming on his face.

"Just because you're good at work doesn't mean you're good with people," Boss chuckled. "Though you don't drive them away, which is why you're still working here."

We were walking around the library for the chat. Fantasy was the first place we passed. Now we were by the horror section. I loathed horror more than any other genre. I didn't want to be scared, I wanted to be comfortable.

The scariest thing I wanted to experience was a thunderstorm.

"I like helping people, just don't understand them all the time," I stated as I looked at a novel about Herobrine.

At least the novel wasn't claiming to be based on a true story. Just the usual group of teenagers being stalked by the ghost story.

"Just don't do anything stupid," Boss said.

10:10 AM

I had just finished setting up the displays. I breathed a sigh of relief and took a look at my work. As it was summer, I had put out books talking about gardening and outdoor sports. I hoped that this helped people have a fun and enjoyable time in the sun.

Boss had forced me to put a few fantasy novels in the displays too. Said people, especially children, would want to read during this time. Why not read about the latest sports craze? He was my boss so I obeyed him.

I smirked as I looked at the position of the fantasy novels. They were slightly obscured by the books I wanted to showcase. It was only a slight win, but at least I could give myself a point.

"You ready?" Boss asked as he walked over to me.

"Always am," I said, turning to smile at him.

I looked as the other librarians stumbled in. It was twenty minutes until the library opened and this was when they decided to show up?

Shaking my head, I walked away.

12:30 PM

"It's in fantasy, not science fiction," I told a patron.

"No, the tale of Harold the Savior is a science fiction novel," the woman said angrily. "It wouldn't make sense for it to be fantasy."

I would've loved to get into a debate about the differences between science fiction and fantasy, but I didn't have the time. James was going off to lunch and I would have to man the checkout area. I took my lunch break after everyone else.

My breakfast held me over until lunchtime and so I didn't feel rushed.

"How about we walk over?" I suggested.

"Fine," she reluctantly agreed.

We walked a short distance from the science fiction section to the fantasy section. A very quick search revealed Harold the Savior. I handed the book to the patron and put a smile on my face. She just took the book and walked away, mumbling.

Some people were so ungrateful.

"Hey, you," a young boy said, waving his hand.

"What do you need help with?" I asked.

It turned out he needed help with a research project. He was trying to start his own garden and didn't feel like any of the books in the display case would help. Some of the research was intricate, and I was glad that the boy had asked me for help.

I doubted that even a botanist could help him with some of the questions. Okay, some of the boy's questions just seemed very far-fetched and I didn't know if the questions even had answers. Or if they were the daydreams of the young.

After the young boy was a writer looking to write a horror story about the Nether. She was smart enough not to venture there herself, but she still needed answers. This one was much easier to do as there were some books that the majority researching the Nether used.

She said thanks as she went to a table to read the books.

3:00 PM

The day was nearly over for me. I always wanted to work longer, but Boss kept on pointing out how I already worked harder than anyone else. He didn't want to wear me down too much because he liked me.

No one else had asked for my help for thirty minutes. This was the only time of day that I would say was boring. I didn't really have that much to do.

I decided to check on overdue books. There weren't many of them as patrons tended to be very good with returning them on time. Usually it took a simple reminder, if there was an overdue book, so that the patron would return them.

I could probably waste my remaining time looking through the overdue book list. As I walked over to where the list was, Boss looked up from his romance novel. He spared me a glance and then went right back to his own personal reading.

The list was in a small room with poor lighting.

I took the list out of its drawer and squinted my eyes so that I could read it better. The lighting in this room really needed to be fixed. Not that I blamed anyone for not doing something about it, the room wasn't used all the much.

Emeralds would be much better spent on other places in the library.

Looking at the list I wondered why people wouldn't return the books. Some of them weren't good literature at all. A lot of them seemed like they could be finished within a day. Maybe the people just lost them?

One of the overdue books caught my attention. Not because the book itself was interesting, some horror story where teenagers were lost in the woods, but because of how long it had been overdue. Not just a few months, like usual, but a few years at least.

In Craftia, people were good about returning their books, so us librarians didn't have to knock on doors most of the time. The address of the person who had checked it out turned to be very close to where the library was.

I could go to them tonight if I had wanted to.

But...I wasn't good with talking to people and so I'd want a night to make sure I didn't accidently insult them.

8:00 PM

I looked at myself in the mirror. I had been practicing what to say for a few hours now. Dinner had been small and simple, so I had plenty of time to practice. Maybe I should've gotten one of my friends to help me.

I didn't know if I was being my usual Jacob self or if I was actually being charming. If what I was being rude or kind. Sometimes it was extremely hard for me to tell the difference.

Tuesday 7:00 AM

I was nervous as I got out of bed. Somehow the sun wasn't as charming as it usually was. I had decided that I would go to the person before going to work today. Better to get this out of the way than dreading it and messing up.

I knew Boss wouldn't mind me having one bad day, but I'd prefer it if the bad day wasn't just because I was nervous about interacting with a person.

It was a good thing that I tended to arrive early so me being late would actually be me arriving on time.

7:30 AM

I rechecked the address as I walked out of my house. I thought of the best ways to get there and how I could quickly go to the library afterwards.

It was a good thing I was leaving so early as there didn't seem to be anyone else walking. Okay, there were a few farmers deciding to get an early start on their day. I didn't blame them as, from what others had said, the heat hadn't let up the other day.

A few had sunburns and I waved at them to hopefully make them feel better.

They waved back. Some looked like they even meant it.

"How are you?" I asked, more to test out my people skills than anything else.

"Hope the sun isn't as hot," one of the sunburned farmers said. "I don't need this sunburn to get any worse."

"At least you can thank the sun for making you look good for once," one of the non-sunburned farmers said.

This sent out a laughter among the others and I joined in. I didn't know if I was supposed to join in or not, but none of them seemed to mind.

"Hot as the Nether these days," one farmer said with a chuckle.

8:00 AM

The person with the overdue book didn't live in the best of places. I could smell things from the neighboring houses and I didn't dwell on what those smells were. I had a hand over my nose and mouth as I knocked on the door.

"Mr. Bagg, I am here to inform you that you have an overdue book," I said and waited.

I didn't think any of the residents would attack me, but the smells... I needed to get out of this place and quick. I thought if I stayed there any longer I would start barfing for the next few days.

"He's not there, hasn't been for a while," a woman's voice said.

I turned to see a well dressed woman that also carried the smells of this place.

"Oh, and the smells are from something he did," the woman replied. "We don't know what and we haven't been able to get rid of it since he did whatever."

"What did he do?" I inquired.

"We don't know and the sounds he made...none of us wanted to be the one who checked him out. They were men sounds so we assume he was a man. When he came out of his house he was always wearing a robe so we could never make out his features."

"Do you know where he went?" I asked her, putting a strained smile on my face.

Then I remembered I was covering up my mouth.

"All we knew is he lived there and suddenly he didn't live there," the woman replied with a shrug. "None of us have tried to go in his house; we don't think it'd be worth it."

While the house itself didn't look bad, the smell was beyond horrible. I wouldn't be surprised that, in a few days, some of the residents suddenly decided to move. Or could they get used to the smell? The woman didn't seem to mind that much.

"Thank you," I replied. "Er...have a nice day?"

9:30 AM

I had put on new clothes after I had returned from Mr. Bagg's place. I didn't want to go to work with such an awful stench on me. I doubted boss would like it either.

I looked in the mirror and thought about the overdue book. It was just one book, the library wouldn't miss it. I could tell Boss and we could get another copy. No big deal. Nothing of importance lost. But I thought of something else, I knew there was only one other option: I would have to find the book myself.

That would mean leaving Craftia. That would mean leaving my huge comfort zone.

I took a deep breath, trying to calm myself down. I counted to ten and then a hundred. I needed to remember my duty. I was a librarian and there was a part of me that couldn't stand not knowing what had happened to that book.

I sighed and resigned myself to what I was about to do. I knew exactly the backpack I would take.

1:00 PM

I jumped as there was a loud knocking on my door. I made sure that I hadn't damaged any items that I was taking on my journey to...I had no idea. I walked to the door and saw Boss. He had the most worried expression I had ever seen on his face, so I made sure to open the door quickly.

"Is everything alright?" Was the first question out of Boss' mouth.

What do I tell him? That I was out to find an overdue book? Would he think I was crazy? Heck, I thought I was crazy.

I explained to him, as clearly as I was capable of doing, that I was looking for a person who had an overdue book. I knew that whatever I was telling him sounded beyond crazy, and I worried what his expression meant.

Throughout my entire explanation a look I had never seen before was on his face.

"Jacob, I never thought you'd be one to do this," Boss replied. "I am proud. You are taking your duties very seriously. Especially concerning overdue books. But if you're not able to find Baggs, we can always order a new copy of the book. I trust you not to do something to endanger your life."

"Why would I do that?" I asked and he put a hand on my shoulder.

"Because once people like you get these urges, strange things happen. I've seen ordinary librarians do...well, what they've done they've sometimes died from. It was something I hoped would never happen to you."

I was then given stories of librarians who had gone to their death over their duties, overdue books mainly, for over an hour. I was growing more nervous as time went by. More and more I did not want to do this. I wanted to just get a new copy of the book.

But with Boss seeming so proud of me...I didn't want to disappoint him.

He finally left. Before he did, he handed me a compass. He said this was his lucky compass he had used back when he was a child. I thought he was going to go after that, but he also said that he would have someone deliver information about Baggs that would be useful for me, and that I should meet this person near the outskirts of town.

Finally, he left.

2:45 PM

I started walking down the street that would take me out of Craftia. A few villagers seemed confused by my presence. I didn't blame them. I was Jacob the Librarian, who never did anything out of the ordinary. I always followed a schedule. I always followed my schedule exactly.

I turned my eyes so they wouldn't look at anyone. I felt everyone judging me. And I thought that they would be laughing about me tonight. Tonight on their comfortable beds that they always slept on. They wouldn't have to worry about getting lost or...or something else. I didn't want to think about that part.

I don't know how long it took me to get out of Craftia. The only thing I knew was that it wasn't enough time. I was leaving the only world I knew.

But, finally, I crossed the line. I took a deep breath as I did so and slowly exhaled once both feet were out of the only place I had ever been.

Turning around I saw some villagers stare at me.

"I'm going after an overdue book," I said awkwardly while the villagers continued to look at me.

The most awkward part of this whole scene had to be the priest who blessed me. Not with a simple blessing, but a long sermon. I only stayed to listen to it because I was so nervous.

It was during the sermon that an exhausted librarian came rushing towards me with books and maps. They were all full of information about what profession Baggs was in and, therefore, what areas he was most likely to frequent.

6:00 PM

I don't know if the evening was colder because I was afraid or if it was actually colder. I was now so far from Craftia that I couldn't see the farms that were around the town. Of course that probably meant I was only a few miles from my home.

In any case, it felt like I was on the opposite side of Minecraftia.

I had stopped a few times to see if I was by an area that Baggs was supposed to have visited. The information Boss had the librarian give to me were highly useful. They were able to take me to an area of which there was an inn.

The people were of a kind I had never seen before. Well, I had seen them but only in books.

One person was drinking coffee while leaning on the outside of the building. The coffee was of a kind I had never encountered before as there was a strange scent to it. The woman drinking it looked at me and waved, her eyes focused more on the sky than me.

I didn't blame her as the sky was a pale shade of red, nearly pinkish. It gave the surroundings a very comforting glow. A mountain in the distance looked particularly beautiful. I wouldn't mind tasting some of that strange coffee and watching the sunset with her.

"You new here?" a man's voice asked and I turned around.

He was short and I was a few inches taller than him. He had a sunburned face so I knew he worked outside.

I thought of how to answer this strange person. Saying I was searching for a person with an overdue book sounded silly. I wanted to make a good impression on these people. Be someone they remembered as a good guy.

"Just taking a walk," I said and it took a few seconds for me to realize how... yeah, that hadn't been a good reply at all.

The short man just laughed loudly.

"You seem far from home," he said, slapping me hard on my lower back. "You traveled far?"

"To me, yes," I told him.

His face was kind and so I decided to tell him who I was and what I was after. I did my best to make searching for an overdue book seem like a heroic adventure. To make it seem like I was doing work that was needed and that I could die.

Death always seemed to make people pay more attention to the story. Was that why the horror genre was so popular?

However, the heroic tale that I thought I was telling wasn't happening. I could tell by the amused grin that the short man had that he thought I was silly.

"So you don't get out much," he said, letting out a soft chuckle. "You have nothing to worry about here. Just...don't tell that story to anyone else. You might find yourself robbed."

6:25 PM

I walked into an inn that seemed like it had good people. But how would I know who was kind and who was wishing harm on me? I hadn't gotten out much as the short man had said. I wouldn't be the best to tell if someone was going to hurt or harm me.

So it was with great apprehension that I got a room in the inn. I looked at the innkeeper's eyes and tried to tell if she wanted me to die or get robbed. She handed me my room key and gave me information on where my room was and what services the inn offered.

Before going to my room I stopped in a little cafe that the inn had. I never drank coffee and so was glad to see that they offered herbal tea.

The tea calmed me down and I decided to write myself a letter so that I would have something to look forward to when I got home. I recounted my great journey to the inn.

A patron looked over my shoulder and asked me if I was from Craftia. When I said yes, he replied that it was only a few miles from here. He also informed me if I wanted to write my life's story that I should do something a little more exciting.

So I had only traveled a few miles from home?

I blushed deeply and tried to make it appear as if the letter was a complete joke. That I totally traveled a lot and this type of thing just happened to amuse me.

The patron walked away laughing. He didn't believe me at all.

Wednesday 7:30 AM

One of the things the inn didn't offer was breakfast. It offered lunch and dinner, but not the meal to start off the day with. When I asked the person at the desk, she just replied that most of the patrons ate breakfast at local diners so the inn had eventually stopped serving breakfast.

This left me outside in the dense morning fog. I held up my hand and could hardly see it. The only reason I was now out here was because I was hungry and that hunger overrode my natural fear instinct.

Almost immediately after walking outside, I started to bump into people. I didn't know how many times I said sorry in a minute, but it must have been a record of some kind. The people I bumped into must have been from around here as they didn't seem to have any problems moving around.

I was too embarrassed to ask them their tricks. I wanted to appear strong so that I wouldn't be taken advantage of.

7:45 AM

I finally managed to find a small cafe. I would've preferred somewhere else, but I just wanted to get out of the fog. I wanted to see where I was for once today and this place seemed decent enough to wait for the fog to clear.

After getting some tea and a pastry, I sat down. Some people were joking about how the fog was bad this morning like it usually was.

"So this is normal?" I asked and instantly wished I had never said anything.

"Yes," an old man said. "Been this way since I was a child. Takes some getting used to, I admit. Took me until I was eighteen to finally figure out how to walk in the fog. All about hearing and knowing the land."

I couldn't learn the land as well as him in just a few hours so if I could just improve my hearing...nope, was still going to wait until the fog cleared.

12:00 PM

The food from breakfast had filled me up for a few hours and I did still have food in my backpack. However, I didn't want to waste it for anything less than an emergency. I didn't want to run out of food before I got back to Craftia.

This left me in the position to constantly be on the lookout for any and all food. I was traveling between towns now so there weren't a lot of options. Actually, there weren't any options currently. I wondered why I was continuing on this journey.

12:30 PM

I was starting to stumble and knew I had to eat something and fast. I wanted to stay on the path, but the cave in the distance seemed to have comforting shade. The shade would allow me to eat a small amount of food outside of the heat of day.

Heading over, I thought I might also take a nap. Walking so much was very tiring, and it was still a few miles until I would reach an area that Baggs was supposed to have frequented. At least if he was anything like his profession, this trip should be interesting and worthwhile. His profession being a wizard that studied magical theories.

As I entered the cave, I was glad that I had been so lucky. I soaked up the shade and sat down once I was far enough in. I took out a small sandwich and started to eat. The food reminded me of home and I imagined that I was just on lunch break from the library.

I imagined some of the other librarians coming out and poking fun at me. They were never cruel and were very helpful when I needed a shoulder to lean on. But when I was feeling fine they didn't mind poking fun at me. One or two seemed to cross a line whenever they talked, though.

After eating I fell asleep.

1:20 PM

I jumped up to a sound. The sound...I had heard about in books. Specifically in books in the horror genre. It took a moment to process, but I finally figured out.

I was about to go out of the cave when I saw that the zombie would get to me before that. I stayed still and hoped that I wouldn't be of too much interest to him. I knew my reflexes weren't good and so it could get to me long before I could even move a muscle for a weapon.

Or at least what I would consider a weapon.

The zombie moaned loudly and I had to stop myself from cringing in case that aggravated the creature more.

My mind was drawing a blank on zombies. I berated myself for not researching them more as that would help in this situation. In my defense, though, I didn't know that I would be facing a zombie one day. In the past, I had never dreamt of leaving the place where I was born. I had never felt a need to explore the entirety of Minecraftia.

I had only felt a need to be a librarian working at one library.

As I was here, I decided to observe the creature before I died. The cave was sheltered from the sun, hence I had decided to come in, and I wondered about the zombie's intelligence. Did it plan to come in here or was it just by accident?

I had to applaud the creature, even if it'd probably be feasting on me soon, if it was intelligent. To set up such a clever trap that an unwary traveler wouldn't think twice about going in. An unwary traveler would see a good place to rest and not think anything of it.

Maybe the villagers around here knew of this zombie cave? If survivors had escaped and legends had spread.

If I could've asked about this cave earlier, if there were legends about this cave, then I wouldn't have stopped by. I would've walked and been happy in the fact that I was still breathing. Of course, finding out would mean asking people. And that wasn't the thing I was good at.

1:35 PM

The zombie still hadn't made a move to eat me. I was both happy and disappointed. If it had eaten me, I wouldn't be waiting for it to do so. And the waiting part was surprisingly boring.

"So what are you waiting for?" I asked the zombie who just continued with its moans. "I have an overdue book to find, so if you're not going to kill me can you give me a sign."

The zombie looked at me confused. Was there a hint of intelligence there? And then it went right back to moaning.

Great. Just great. I'm in the most boring life or death situation ever. If I ever got out of this alive, I was going to change a few details to make it sound exciting. When the zombie moaned again, I let out a loud sigh.

"Oh, you're moaning again? You've never done that before!" I said sarcastically and wonder where that came from.

I wasn't a people person, but I didn't like to say rude things at any time. Maybe the fear of death was doing something to me. Maybe I had given up on life?

No, that wasn't it. I just didn't care. Somehow I had entered a form of meditation I had never known existed. Maybe this is why people went on grand adventures. But to get to this state of peace was just not worth it.

2:30 PM

Again the zombie moaned and I got angry. For some reason my state of peace had gone into a full blown rage.

"Just kill me already!" I said and jumped up.

The zombie quickly moved towards me, maybe it was because I was moving that he suddenly showed interest, and I started to dance. Actually, I didn't know if it was dancing or not. I didn't dance much. At least not as much as other people did.

I twirled around and started laughing. I added more movements to what I was sure was going to be my final moments on Minecraftia. I got into whatever dance I was doing and added words. My song turned into random words set to a tune.

I stopped when I heard a strange sound. Wait? Was the zombie laughing?

I started dancing once it let out another moan and its moan turned into a chuckle. After a few minutes it started to clap. This spurred me on to make a dangerous decision: to make my way out of the cave.

I was out of the cave when the zombie let out a loud yell. I shivered and stood just a few feet away from the entrance, the sun stopping the zombie from chasing after me. Was it mad that its prey was gone or that its toy was running away?

It could've killed me so easily...did it just like to be amused more than it liked to eat?

4:45 PM

I breathed a huge sigh of relief when I saw a farm. One of the farmers turned to look at me. There must not be many people around here as I didn't see many travelers besides myself traveling this way. There was a reason the farmer was a little surprised at a traveler.

"Yo!" she shouted, wiping sweat off of her forehead. "What you doing around here?"

I hadn't yet worked out how to turn the zombie incident into something exciting, so I left out that part of my journey. I told her all about looking for an overdue book and did my best to make the whole venture seem daring and exciting.

She laughed a few times, so I had to pause until she stopped. Her laughter was annoying, as it seemed to turn my entire existence into a joke. But there was something pleasant about hearing laughter after being stuck in that cave with a zombie.

"So, Baggs?" she asked and seemed to spend a little time thinking about the name.

I asked her if she knew him and she seemed to only know stories about him. Rumors that had spread quickly. As I was about to leave, she said that she knew where he was supposed to be currently.

"I have only one request," she said with a grin. "Take me with you."

Take her with me? What would she have to add besides knowing where the mysterious Baggs was? I could find out that information if I wanted to. Then I realized I wasn't an experienced traveler and having someone with me should help to keep me safe.

Was she dangerous and I just couldn't see it, though?

"Um...don't you have work you're supposed to do?" I asked.

I had nearly died earlier, I guess I'd take another chance.

"I can get Ted to take care of my portion until I return. Shouldn't be long," she replied.

She packed up quickly and only then did I find out her name. Her name was Lucy.

Thursday 8:30 AM

Our bellies were both full from a good sized breakfast. Lucy had brought enough supplies to last us a few weeks, though we both doubted our search for Baggs would last that long. My companion knew the area well it seemed.

There was only one problem that seemed huge to me at the moment, but maybe I'd laugh at it later. Lucy was very fond of jokes and taking things lightly. It seemed that every chance she got she would say something. Sometimes laughing at her own jokes that she found hilarious, but I just didn't get.

Maybe I needed a sense of humor like she said, or maybe I just don't get humor. In my defense, someone laughing an hour at the word oranges is...strange.

Currently, she was asking me to answer 'Why did the zombie cross the road?'

I had been holding out answering her for five minutes, but finally fell victim to her.

"Why?" I said with a sigh.

"To get to the other side," Lucy replied. "We're going to need to hurry up and find Baggs. Even I found that joke bad."

"So you told that joke even though you knew it was bad?"

"Yeah, so?"

I just shook my head and continued walking.

9:05 AM

Lucy had been silent for a few minutes and I felt better than I had in awhile. I could finally concentrate on my own thoughts and decide how I would approach the elusive Baggs. I tried to think up words and phrases that people would usually use to talk to others with.

I didn't want to ask my companion as...yeah, just no.

"You see that?" Lucy asked and I turned in her direction.

I shook my head and turned away quickly, I figured this was one of her practical jokes. Well... she had never done any practical jokes to me, but she looked like a practical joker.

"Come on, look!" Lucy hissed so I looked again.

And there he was. Or it was. It had been regarded as no more than an urban legend by most and now, here it was. Lucy was silent, but she mouthed the word: Herobrine.

I was frozen in place and I longed for the other day with the zombie. At least then all I had to do was dance and sing. But for Herobrine? Maybe I should learn more about him when I got back or never go outside of Craftia.

If I lived, that was.

"Do you know how to get rid of him?" I asked Lucy and she just shook her head in reply.

"Maybe if we wish really hard he'll go away," she said after a few minutes.

I groaned. How could she joke in a time like this? We were about to die and all she could do was make one more joke. We should be looking for a way out, not laughing as we did.

Lucy then tried teaching me some quick breathing exercises. I tried to follow her instructions, I really did, but fear always made me mess up.

"Let's just walk and see if he doesn't follow," Lucy said with a strained grin.

I didn't want to move, but... I had to. What if it was like the zombie and all I had to do was start moving?

I nodded and we started to walk. We talked about our jobs and why we liked them. It turned out she liked to catalogue plants in her spare time and was going to inherit the farm she worked on when her father died. It seemed she liked adventure from time to time.

Hence, she had joined my quest.

We got into a little debate when it turned out that I didn't like adventures at all, and I was only venturing so far from home because of the overdue book. She tried to convince me that I did want adventure or else I wouldn't have come this far for an overdue book.

11:00 AM

It had been some time since I had last glanced over my shoulder to check for the figure of Herobrine. For awhile now, I had been able to admire the countryside. Especially the mountains in the distance. Some snow was still on the mountains even though it was a little late in the year for that to be the case.

"Hey, maybe I should invite you around the campfire one night to tell ghost stories," Lucy said cheerfully. "How about the story where the Librarian hunts for an overdue book for all of time because he can never find it?"

"I'm trying to stay calm," I replied and turned when I heard a noise.

But, no, it wasn't Herobrine.

"Not about you, silly," Lucy said with a laugh. "If it was about you, the Librarian would never leave his house."

I let out a sigh to try and hide a chuckle.

Soon we tried to debate if Herobrine would ever come back. We decided that that was unlikely.

12:05 PM

Lucy and I prepared a small picnic. We sat in a grove of trees. She had brought some bread and I provided some water. We had drank all our milk during the morning. Milk could go bad quickly and we both thought that the journey would be short.

Though my companion referred to the journey as an outing. Like it was just meaningless to her. I wanted to shake my head whenever I thought about her viewpoint.

"Nothing to worry about," Lucy said. "We'll find Baggs and you can go back home. And I can go back to sweating in the fields every day."

"And I can stay in the shade," I said, thinking of the library and how I never wanted to leave it.

I heard some twigs break and turned slowly. I expected a small animal, instead I saw a human-like creature with pure white eyes. Empty and soulless. It was Herobrine.

Before I could think, I was standing up and Lucy was holding me.

I turned to Lucy to see if she had any words of comfort. But her face was pure white and that made me even more worried. If she lost hope, then what hope could I have?

"Is my skin the same color as his eyes?" she asked and I laughed.

Good, she was still in there.

"Run?" I asked and then we were moving.

12:20 PM

I spent the majority of my days looking through books and helping people find information. My brain held vast amounts of data, though I was by no means the smartest person on the planet.

But brain power didn't help when you needed to do something physical.

It had only been a short time running, but my lungs felt like they were going to burst. I could imagine some of the library patrons telling me that this was the reason that I should work out. They were saying how one never knows when Herobrine will chase after you; therefore, you must always be prepared.

I yelled at them asking how I was supposed to have known that Herobrine would ever be after me. I never even knew I would be leaving Craftia.

"And I'm the crazy one?" Lucy asked with a grin.

I had said that out loud? Yeah, there was no recovering from that one.

We found a large boulder to hide behind to momentarily catch our breath. We had left behind nearly all our food and now we were far off our intended path. I tried thinking quickly and came up with a blank to where we were. I had studied the map very carefully and so it was probably due to stress that I couldn't think right now.

I asked Lucy if she knew where we were, but she had gotten too confused with all the running. I guess we had only been thinking about getting away earlier and not having a specific destination.

So the current plan was to keep on running. Once we got a few minutes to regain our breath.

We both yelled out as Herobrine appeared behind us. Whoa! He's fast…

Then I remembered something: Herobrine was supposed to run much faster than any villager could and it hadn't been running faster than us this entire time.

As Lucy and I started to run, a horrible thought passed through my mind: Herobrine was merely toying with us.

1:00 PM

Lucy and I had stopped a few times. Herobrine was kind enough to let us take a breather now and again. Sometimes I swear his twitching figure was laughing at us.

"We can't run forever," I told Lucy in a rare moment of bravery. "We have to do something."

"We can't fight it," Lucy replied as she shook her head. "No one has been able to. Either because Herobrine runs away or because some have died fighting him. Though the latter is more urban legend than anything else."

"So we, what, scare him?"

"That might be hard to do."

Yeah, scaring a creature of legend would be beyond hard to do. Moving mountains would be easier. Then I had an idea, but I didn't know if I was brave enough to go through with it. It would take me some place...I didn't know if I was prepared to go.

"Lucy, do we have any obsidian?" I asked and she just stared at me.

1:30 PM

Both of us looked at each other. Then we looked to see if Herobrine was around.

I looked in front of us to the portal to the Nether. It was ignited and all that was left was for us to enter it.

"You know this is stupid, right?" Lucy asked, trying to appeal to reason again. "We could die in there."

"Or we will just go in and then come back out with Herobrine gone," I explained again. "It'll just be so confused that it'll give up."

"You got the confused part right."

Maybe Lucy was right. This plan was stupid. I wasn't prepared to travel outside of Craftia, much less into the Nether. And my only companion didn't feel safe with this idea.

I looked behind me to see if Herobrine was behind us. It wasn't. Maybe it had gone away and I didn't have to go into the Nether. Maybe it was waiting for me to close the portal just so killing us would be more fun. I gulped and stepped through the portal.

The feeling of going through the portal seemed to last a lifetime. It was if I could see into things and myself. I could see how Lucy saw me and I could see...no, I could feel fire.

I screamed and suddenly I was in the Nether. I fell down as I tried to recover as much as I could. Lucy soon followed and she appeared dizzy, though she didn't react like I had.

"So this is the Nether," Lucy said, acting brave or maybe she really was. "Needs some touching up."

We both jumped as a random fire sprouted on the ground near us. A hop, skip, and jump away was some lava. In the distance was more lava. I shivered, although it was far from cold down here.

10:30 PM

We had spent awhile in the Nether and figured that Herobrine was most likely gone by now. It had probably picked another victim. But there was a new problem.

From what I knew about the Nether, places in it connected to the world I had been born in. Though figuring out what was where was another matter. Lucy and I had already been lost, now we were even more so.

Even Lucy's humor seemed to have died off. She had even grown quiet and that was the worst part. If even she couldn't laugh at our situation, how could I stay sane?

Finally, we found a place we could rest for the night. I was tired as my body had never been pushed to such extremes before. The running was one thing, but navigating the Nether had been something else entirely.

We ate a small dinner as we had left the majority of our food at the picnic, and we both didn't know how long it would take getting out of the Nether, never mind how long it would take getting home.

"Don't heroes usually have one sleep and the other keep watch?" Lucy asked.

"I...I don't tend to read those kinds of stories, but I think so. Why?" I replied.

"You should keep first watch then."

Friday 5:30 AM

I had trouble sleeping during the night, so did Lucy. We had moved around a few times just so we would feel safe. But could we even be safe down here?

And to make matters even worse, Lucy talked during her sleep. She made bad jokes in her sleep! I guess I hadn't noticed it before as I was too comfy sleeping. But now...with the Nether and her jokes not taking a break, I was going to go mad soon. I was more than sure of it.

Now neither of us could sleep as a sound woke us up. We instantly turned toward the sound and saw...I tried to think of the word. Lucy thought of the words first: magma cubes.

The sound they made was distinctive and I wondered where I had learned about the sound from.

The magma cubes moved by hopping and I found the movement hypnotic. Or maybe it was because I was so afraid that my mind was calming me down however it could.

In any case, I watched as the magma cubes came toward us. Lucy's breathing was increasing and I could tell that our calmness would end if either of us lost it for even a second.

I looked around to see where there was to run. I saw something in the distance and pointed at it to Lucy. I couldn't tell what it was but at least it was a destination.

"You don't know what it is?" Lucy said without any emotion to her voice.

With that we started off. I felt one of the cubes singe my leg. I stumbled.

I turned my fall into a roll and my companion finally helped me up. I took a moment to catch my breath before we both continued to run as we heard the cubes.

9:00 AM

"We are there!" I shouted in frustration.

Being chased by the magma cubes, as well as other denizens of the Nether, had made me lose some contents of my backpack. I fell and stumbled numerous times while Lucy merely stumbled. Both of us wore some cuts from the enemies we had run from.

During that time, I had lost the rest of the obsidian I had been carrying. Lucy had already ranted to me about that and now she was quiet on the topic. Either because she was saving her energy or she found arguing with me on the topic more than useless.

"Right above us...maybe we can find some obsidian around here..." I said hopefully and Lucy just laughed.

But it wasn't a friendly laugh, it felt like the sound was a weapon. For a moment, I was unsure whether to fear her laughter or the Nether more.

Hours and hours had taken us to figuring out where we wanted to go and now we were stuck.

"Yeah, I'm sure there's a lot of obsidian around here waiting to be picked up," Lucy finally said. "And, even if there was some, what about the creatures guarding it?"

I wanted to say she was wrong, that I was stronger than she thought, but I knew she was right. I wasn't a fighter and I probably wouldn't live long enough to be a hero. I never wanted to be a hero on a grand adventure, I just wanted to be safe in Craftia.

Why did I think this search for an overdue book would be easy?

"If we ever get out of this alive, remind me never to listen to you again," Lucy told me.

"No problem, I won't travel outside Craftia again," I said with what I hoped sounded like a laugh.

3:00 PM

The day had become boring once we had figured out how to stay alive. We had incidents of near death, but the only bad thing to happen from those had been Lucy finally finding her sense of humor again.

"Hoppity hop!" Was Lucy's new phrase she said whenever we were chased by magma cubes.

For fun, we harassed zombie pigmen whenever we saw them. It had taken two times running into them before we figured out that they wouldn't attack us. They were the only thing I found funny. I would spend minutes looking at them until Lucy pulled me away.

"So this is it?" Lucy said as we sat during a rare moment of peace in the Nether. "I won't be going back to my farm and you won't be going back to your library. You leaving anyone behind?"

"Some family...Boss...few sort of friends..." I said as I listed off people I knew.

"No!" she said with a laugh. "Like a girlfriend or boyfriend."

I wasn't much into relationships, the only relationship I had was with my work. That love was enough for me. Besides, starting a relationship meant interacting with people. I wasn't too good in that area.

"No," I said and ate one of the remaining fruits. "I don't have anyone like that."

"Doesn't that bother you?"

"Why should it?"

Lucy didn't seem to be able to answer that. I knew that a lot of people didn't understand my choice. Sometimes people even questioned me on the topic. I would explain it to her, but... it wasn't exactly the thing I'd like to talk about before I died.

I don't know if it'd be on my top ten list of conversations that shouldn't happen before I die. But it would be up there.

"I don't know, just seems odd," Lucy said. "So what is your biggest regret? Mine is not going into standup when I had the chance."

"You really wanted to torture people with your jokes?" I teased and she gave me a playful punch on the shoulder.

We both laughed and looked around for any enemies. None came at us.

"So what is yours?" Lucy asked.

"You're going to laugh at me," I said slowly, embarrassed. "But...not finding the overdue book. I ventured outside of Craftia and I'm going to die without even finding it."

"Maybe you can do that in the next life. Figured you book lovers would just spend eternity reading books. Playing pranks on authors you didn't like. You know, what you wanted to do while alive."

I saw her smile and could tell that she was joking.

"What do you plan to do if you become a ghost?" I asked her.

"You joking? Of course I'm going to spend my afterlife playing pranks on people," Lucy said with a grin. "Maybe even make people think a house or two is haunted by an evil spirit."

What had I expected Lucy to say? She had such a light-hearted spirit that she wouldn't use her next life to do something meaningful, she'd use it to have fun. And she did deserve that. I had led her to the Nether with no way out.

"Maybe we could have a ghost rivalry?" I asked nervously.

"You mean like who gets to haunt what house?" Lucy replied. "Or like who ge-"

We stopped as we heard movement. I looked towards the sound and decided not to run anymore. If I was going to die, I was going to die.

I saw a wither skeleton walking slowly towards us. It had a backpack on its back and a sword in its hand. Sound seemed to be coming from its mouth, but it didn't sound like any I had heard before. I also smelled a distinctive scent from it...but I couldn't place where I had smelled something like it before.

"Fight?" Lucy asked me.

"Yes," I replied and looked at the wither skeleton much braver than I felt.

When the skeleton was standing mere feet in front of us, it puts down its sword and held up its hands. It was peaceful? I looked over to Lucy in confusion, she just shook her head in confusion.

"You're from up there," the skeleton said and pointed up. "I went up there one time. I wore a disguise so others wouldn't know what I was. It was a poor disguise, so I had to hide away a majority of the time. The disguise also had another problem."

The smell. That's what it had to be.

"Baggs, you're...not human," I said and I swore he grinned at me.

He went on to say that it was only because of the stench that he went back to the Nether sooner than he had intended to. He didn't want to draw attention to himself. He feared if others knew what he was, that some adventurer would try to disrupt his peaceful vacation.

"You mentioned an overdue book," Baggs stated. "Are you from Craftia? I went to a library there one day, before my disguise started to stink, and took a book. I'm not too familiar with your customs."

So that's why he hadn't returned the book. How could I expect someone from the Nether to understand things that I took for granted? I didn't know how to deal with people, but I knew the basics.

"So no libraries down here?" Lucy said, trying to lighten the mood.

5:00 PM

Finally, Baggs stopped talking about why there weren't any libraries down in the Nether. I had tried to stay focused as the heat became more than a little overwhelming.

"It's nice here, but can't you help us out?" Lucy asked.

It seemed Baggs was highly embarrassed as he spent a few minutes saying sorry. He handed me the book, and I could see it was in relatively good condition. Good condition considering it had been down in the Nether.

"Follow me, I will take you to where I used to go up there," Baggs said.

Following him, I felt much safer, especially as he knew paths that had been completely hidden from us before. I looked to Lucy in amazement and she was just smiling. She was talking to Baggs about her farm and he replied to her.

I chimed in every now and again to clarify things, but I mostly stayed silent. I knew if there was one person that would mess this up it would be me. I knew how I could think I was doing a good job, but still make people angry from time to time.

What Lucy and myself didn't need right now was our one way out
gone.

I tried to remember where Baggs was taking us on the off chance I
ever returned. Though the only plans I had were to stick to my usual
routine and never leave Craftia again. I really didn't need to get into
all this trouble again.

Baggs set up the portal as I tried to calm myself. I couldn't believe that someone from the Nether would really help us. This had to be some elaborate trap. A few times, as the wither skeleton prepared the portal, he made some odd noises.

He sounded like he was cackling and he had to reassure us that he was merely sighing. Someone with a more adventurous spirit would think about staying to observe this strange creature more. I wasn't a hero and I felt no guilt about going.

"If I go up there then I will be sure of visiting you," Baggs said.

I merely nodded in agreement so that the wither skeleton wouldn't think about turning back on his word.

As I stepped through the portal, I worried that this was a trap. That this was...not going to end well. That Baggs had pretended to accidently take the book, but had really been waiting for a librarian to come after it. And when one did, he would have fun.

I breathed in the fresh air of Minecraftia. I took a few deep breaths and turned to Lucy, who had gone through right alongside me. I was so overjoyed that I couldn't speak for a few minutes.

How can I properly describe how I was feeling to someone who hasn't been to the Nether? I thought I was going to die in the Nether and, instead, I was helped by the most unlikely of creatures.

"We can say we've been to the Nether and back," Lucy said after a few minutes.

"For an overdue book," I said with a grin on my face.

Lucy shook her head and I tried to figure out where we were. We were in the mountains and I was unsure if any town was nearby. My companion started walking, and I followed her just in case she knew where she was going.

I had spent the last two hours reading on my porch. Reading about gardening so that maybe I could start a garden later. I had been looking around town for a good place to buy seeds. I wanted people to walk by my house and stop for a moment to look at delicious treats growing.

While reading the gardening book, I thought back about my adventure. The growing heat of the day was much different than the coldness of the mountains. The coldness that made me wish for the heat of the Nether.

Lucy and I had found a traveler who was more than willing to show us to a town. From the town, it had been a lengthy journey to get her back to her farm and me to Craftia.

I sipped some tea that was on a table beside me and thought about how good it was to not have to worry about food. I could just go into my kitchen and get what I wanted. I didn't have to ration out food. And if I needed more food?

There were places nearby that sold what I liked.

I didn't have to worry, and it was strange to think adventurers liked that kind of thing. I had firmly decided to only travel outside of Craftia to visit Lucy now and again. I wouldn't venture out just to get into danger again.

Or maybe I wouldn't visit Lucy. A simple trip had been what had led me to the Nether, after all.

I got up to get some more tea and to finally throw away Boss' 'lucky' compass.

Can You Help Me Out?

Thanks for reading all the way through. I hope that you enjoyed this book. As a new writer, it is hard to get started; it is difficult to find an audience that wants to read my books. There are millions of books out there and sometimes it is super hard to find one specific book. But that's where you come in! You can help other readers find my books by leaving a simple review. It doesn't have to be a lengthy or well written review; it just has to be a few words and then click on the stars. It would take less than 5 minutes.

Seriously, that would help me so much, you don't even realize it. Every time I get a review, good or bad, it just fills me with motivation to keep on writing. It is a great feeling to know that somewhere out there, there are people who actually enjoy reading my books. Anyway, I would super appreciate it, thanks.

If you see new books from me in the future, you will know that I wrote them because of your support. Thank you for supporting my work.

Special thanks again to previous readers and reviewers. Thank you for encouraging me to keep writing. I'll do my best to provide high quality books for you all.

My Other Books

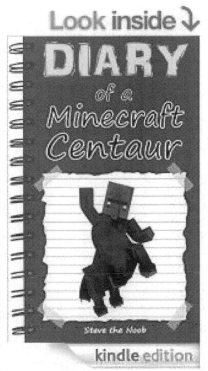

Check Out My Author Page
Steve the Noob

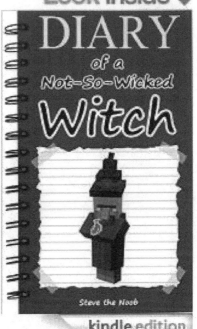

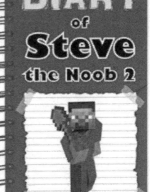

My Awesome List of Favorite Readers and Reviewers

Jewel Shine

Minoscreeperslayer

RainbowCreeper

Sang Chul Choi

Misahti

Panisara W.

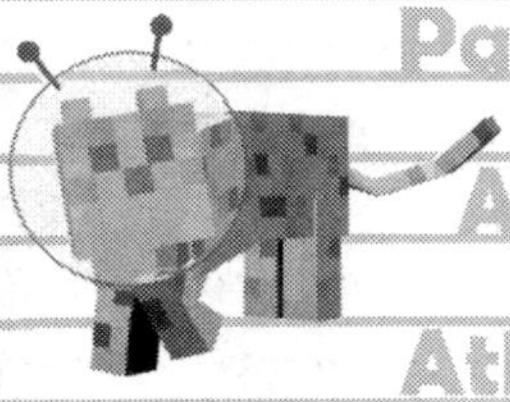

Astro Cat

AthanEnder

betsy

akaherobrine

James

Xaxier Edwards

leann xiao

Awesomeguy27

IsaBear556

Emma Hogan

Brandon Kim

Venu Gopal

Kathy

Yuan Cui

Sreekant Gottimukkala

Made in the USA
Lexington, KY
14 November 2016